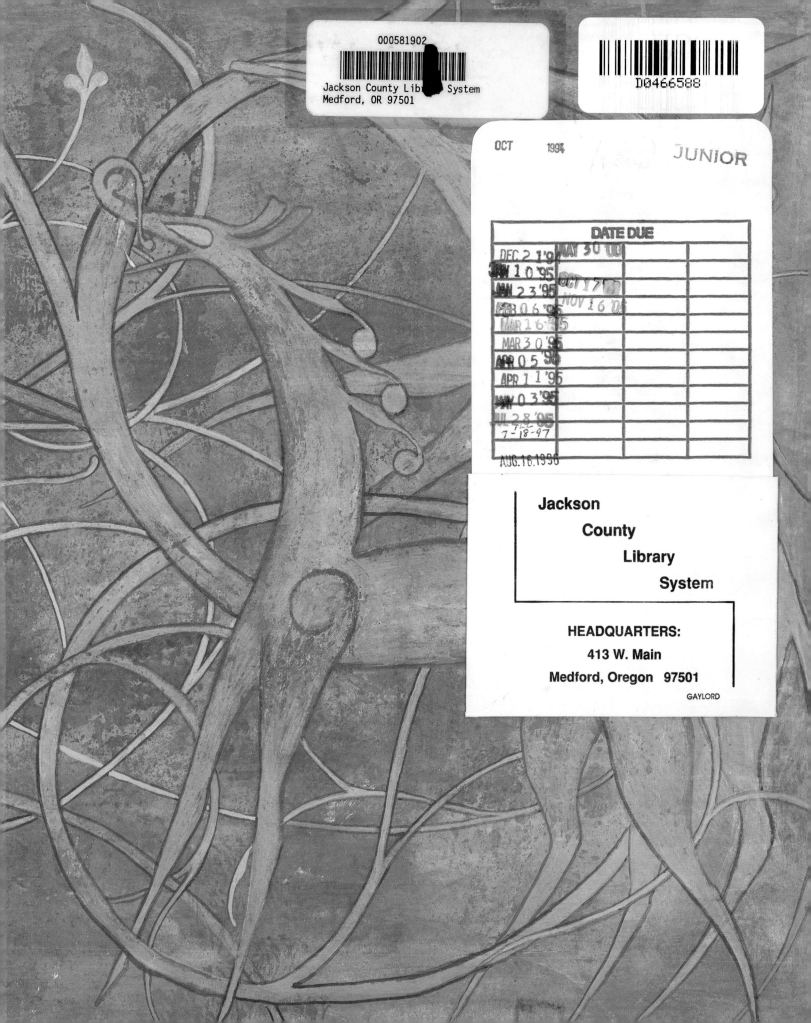

STOLEN THUNDER

◆ A NORSE MYTH ◆

Retold by SHIRLEY CLIMO
Illustrated by ALEXANDER KOSHKIN

CLARION BOOKS / *New York*

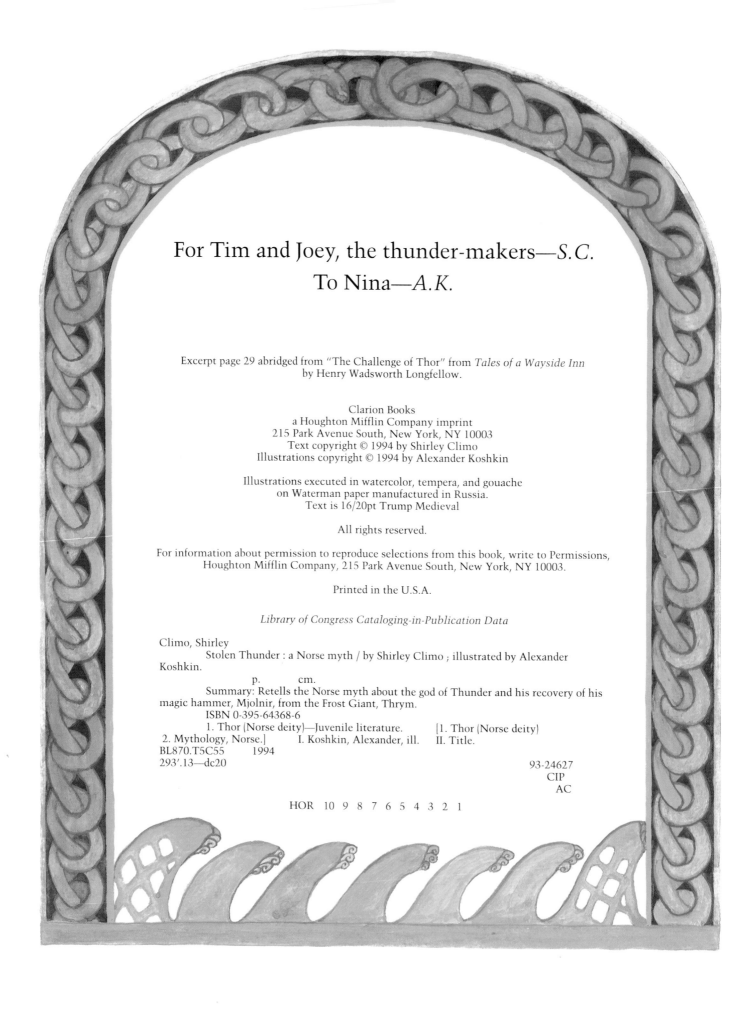

For Tim and Joey, the thunder-makers—*S.C.*
To Nina—*A.K.*

Excerpt page 29 abridged from "The Challenge of Thor" from *Tales of a Wayside Inn*
by Henry Wadsworth Longfellow.

Clarion Books
a Houghton Mifflin Company imprint
215 Park Avenue South, New York, NY 10003
Text copyright © 1994 by Shirley Climo
Illustrations copyright © 1994 by Alexander Koshkin

Illustrations executed in watercolor, tempera, and gouache
on Waterman paper manufactured in Russia.
Text is 16/20pt Trump Medieval

For information about permission to reproduce selections from this book, write to Permissions,
Houghton Mifflin Company, 215 Park Avenue South, New York, NY 10003.

Printed in the U.S.A.

Library of Congress Cataloging-in-Publication Data

Climo, Shirley
        Stolen Thunder : a Norse myth / by Shirley Climo ; illustrated by Alexander
Koshkin.
                p.   cm.
        Summary: Retells the Norse myth about the god of Thunder and his recovery of his
magic hammer, Mjolnir, from the Frost Giant, Thrym.
        ISBN 0-395-64368-6
        1. Thor (Norse deity)—Juvenile literature.   [1. Thor (Norse deity)
2. Mythology, Norse.]   I. Koshkin, Alexander, ill.   II. Title.
BL870.T5C55   1994
293'.13—dc20
                                                                        93-24627
                                                                        CIP
                                                                        AC

                        HOR   10 9 8 7 6 5 4 3 2 1

ong ago, in the morning of time, there lived a people called the Norse. Their lands lay far to the north, where the cold winter stays too long and the warm summer leaves too soon. In this world, the Norse believed, lived many strange beings, both wonderful and terrible.

The universe, their storytellers explained, was supported by a great green ash tree. In the highest branches of this World Tree, above the clouds, was the walled city of Asgard, home of the gods. Father Odin, wise and gray-bearded, was their ruler. It was he who scattered the stars in the sky and kept the sun awake on summer evenings. Most of the gods and goddesses were powerful and good, although among them was a young mischief-maker named Loki.

Limbs in the center of the tree supported Midgard, or Middle Earth, where ordinary human folk lived. To visit the mortals, the gods and goddesses traveled down a many-colored bridge. When a rainbow arched across the sky, people said,

"Look! A god is coming down to call on us."

In shadowy caverns beneath the earth lived the dwarfs. Although they crafted marvelous treasures from gold and silver, they themselves were mean and bad-tempered. When people heard echoes in caves, they said,

"Listen! The dwarfs are quarreling again."

The branches of the World Tree spread to the edge of the earth, to icebound cliffs that rimmed the chilly sea. This was Jotunheim, land of the giants, and fierce Thrym the frost giant was king. It was he who whistled up the howling winds of winter. When a storm raged, people shivered and said,

"Brrr! Feel the breath of Thrym the Frost King!"

The giants envied the gods and schemed to seize the shining palaces of Asgard. But first the giants had to overcome Thor, the Thunder-maker.

Thor was the biggest and strongest of all the gods. He sped across the heavens in a chariot pulled by two goats with twisted horns, swinging his fearful hammer over his head. This hammer, named Mjolnir, was magic. It never missed its mark, always returned to the hand that threw it, and was so hot that even Thor wore iron gloves to hold it.

When Thor drove his chariot across the sky, sparks flew from beneath the wheels, and people on earth gasped and said,

"See the lightning!"

When Thor hurled his hammer, clouds cracked open with a roar. Then those below trembled and cried,

"Hear the thunder!"

Giants dared not challenge the gods as long as Thor had Mjolnir. At night, he slept with it close beside him. At daybreak, as soon as he had buckled his strength-giving belt and pulled on his iron gloves, Thor reached under the bedclothes for his hammer. But one morning . . .

"W here's Mjolnir?" roared Thor.

He flung off his bearskin cover, tipped up his bed, and peered under it, but found only a frightened mouse.

Thor tugged at his beard in disbelief. "A hammer cannot walk on one leg. Mjolnir cannot fly by itself. It cannot vanish unless . . . unless . . . Rascal!" Thor shouted. "Robber!"

Loki thrust his head in the doorway. "Whatever happened," he said, "I'm not to blame."

"Mjolnir has disappeared!" Thor bellowed. "And you took it!"

"I was asleep, minding my own dreams, until your shouts woke me," protested Loki. "I didn't touch your fiery hammer." He wriggled his fingers. "Look! My hands aren't even red."

"Who else would play such a prank?" demanded Thor, dangling Loki by his collar like a fish on a line.

"Put . . . me . . . down, Thor," Loki panted. "Listen!"

"I have already heard all your excuses."

"Don't listen to *me*," pleaded Loki. "Just listen!"

Holding Loki with one hand, Thor cupped the other to his ear. From far away came a rumble, like boulders knocking about in an iron pot.

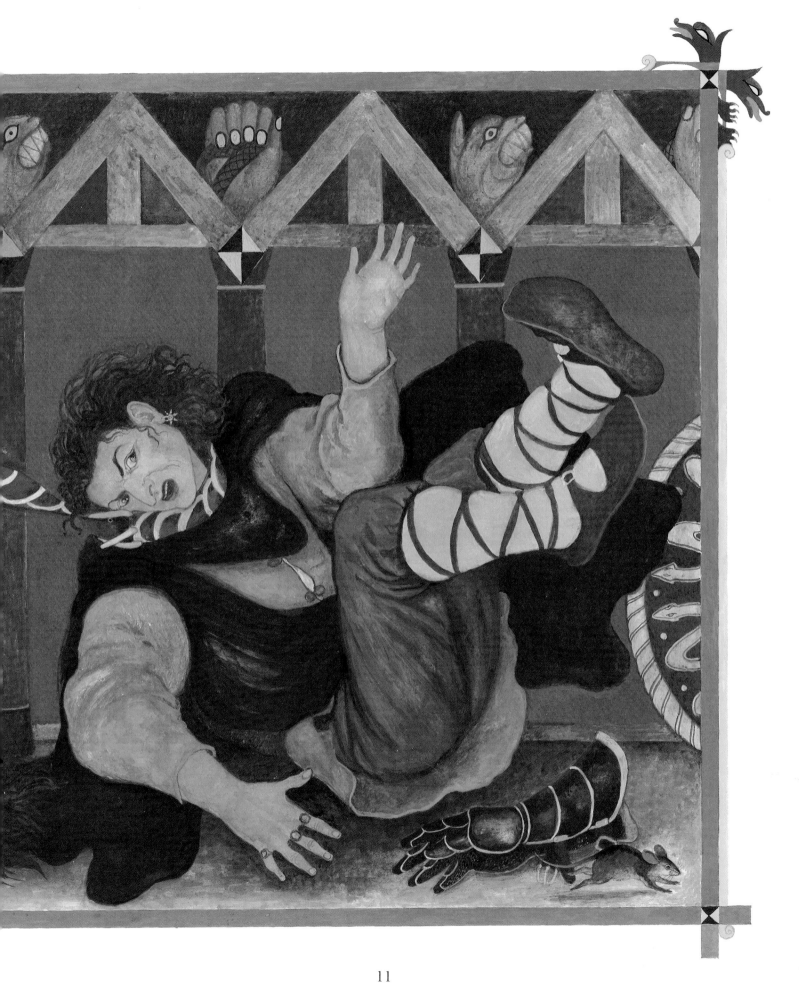

"That's Mjolnir's voice!" Thor howled. "Someone has stolen my thunder!" He dropped Loki. "I will get Mjolnir back if I have to turn the whole world upside down and inside out!"

"And alarm everyone in it!" said Loki, brushing himself off. "And alert the thief? But if I helped . . ."

"You!" Thor snorted. "What could you do?"

"No one has stolen my wits," said Loki smugly. "If I borrow the goddess Freya's falcon cloak, I can fly below and search out your hammer."

"And then I shall smash the wretch who stole it!" shouted Thor, stamping his foot so hard all five hundred forty doors in his palace slammed shut.

"Hush!" warned Loki. "The fewer who know Mjolnir is missing, the better."

Thor and Loki found Freya brushing the two sleek cats that pulled her chariot. Freya was the goddess of love and beauty, and she greeted the two gods with a dazzling smile. But she frowned when Loki asked to borrow her falcon cloak.

"You might fly too close to the sun and scorch it," Freya objected.

"This favor is not for Loki," Thor said. "Nor is it for me alone. It is for the safety of all the gods."

Freya sighed. "Then I must," she said, and handed Loki her falcon cloak.

Loki pulled the feathered hood over his head, spread his arms, and soared through the sky above Asgard. To those below, he looked like a falcon in flight.

Loki was certain of Mjolnir's whereabouts. Still, he glided down the rainbow bridge and hovered over

Midgard, admiring his reflection in a millpond. No mortal here could handle Thor's hammer, and no dwarf had reason to. Loki dawdled, turning a midair somersault, then flew over the mountaintops to Jotunheim.

Spring did not come to the dismal land of the giants. Icicles never melted, and snow always clung to the bald mountains. On top of the tallest crag sprawled Thrym the Frost King, trimming his fingernails with his hunting knife.

"Aha!" Thrym exclaimed, pointing the knife at Loki. "A crow has flown in for supper!"

"A falcon," said Loki indignantly.

"Crow or falcon," Thrym replied. "One tastes like another."

Loki pulled off his hood. "I am a messenger from the gods."

"A fine-feathered errand runner!" The giant snickered. "And how goes life in Asgard?"

"Terrible," moaned Loki. "Thor has lost his hammer."

"How careless!" Thrym said.

"Someone stole it," Loki explained.

Thrym sneered, showing teeth sharp as a wolf's. "Think of that!"

"I am . . ." said Loki, searching for words, "I am thinking how clever the thief must be."

The giant leaned toward him. "More clever than a god?"

"More clever than all gods put together!" Loki said. "I'd like to meet such a sharp-witted fellow."

"You are talking to him!" boasted Thrym. "Watch!"

The frost giant heaved rocks aside and sent them rolling down the mountain. Then, with his knife, he dug deep into the frozen ground, and pulled out Mjolnir. The handle sizzled and steamed when his icy fingers touched it.

"Thor's hammer!" gasped Loki.

"My hammer," corrected Thrym. "I blew a little blizzard through Thor's window last night."

"Without wakening him?"

"He never missed a snore, but he did shake and shiver so that Mjolnir fell to the floor. I reached in . . ." The giant twirled the hammer. "And now *I* am Thunderlord."

"But surely a mighty giant has no need for such a little hammer . . ."

"No tricks!" The giant scowled. "Mjolnir is mine."

"Perhaps you would trade it for chests of gold," Loki offered, rubbing his hands, "or sacks of jewels."

"Not for anything," declared Thrym. "Or for anyone, either—save for lovely Freya."

"Freya!"

"Mjolnir can be Thor's again if Freya will be mine."

"And if Freya will not?" asked Loki.

Thrym threw the hammer. Nearby mountains split apart and the World Tree trembled. When the hammer had returned to his hand, the king of the frost giants declared, "Then take this message to the gods: Beware!"

Loki straggled back to Asgard on drooping wings. First he gave Freya her cloak. Then he told Thor that Mjolnir was in Thrym's hands.

Thor's face flushed as red as his beard. "Scoundrel!" he bellowed. "I'll teach him!"

"You forget." Loki tugged on Thor's sleeve. "Without Mjolnir you cannot battle the giants."

"I have my belt of strength!"

"Thrym would tear it like a spiderweb," the younger god argued, adding, "but he is willing to bargain."

Thor clenched his fists. "What does that scheming giant want?"

"Not what," said Loki. "Who. Thrym wants Freya for his bride."

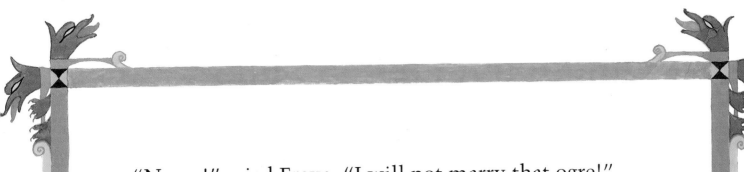

"Never!" cried Freya. "I will not marry that ogre!"

"Thrym is terrible beyond all telling," Loki admitted. "Still, Asgard is lost unless you go to Jotunheim."

Freya began to weep, crying tears of purest gold.

Loki looked at Thor. "Unless," he said slyly, "Thor himself goes as Thrym's bride."

"Me!" exclaimed Thor. "What nonsense!"

"Disguised as Freya you might recover your hammer," said Loki.

"Dress up in women's clothes?" Thor shouted. "All Asgard will laugh at me! Not by my beard!"

"Not even for Mjolnir?" asked Loki.

"Not even for me?" asked Freya.

Thor groaned. "Send word to Jotunheim to prepare for a wedding they will never forget."

Still grumbling, Thor put on bridal linens. He covered his hairy legs and knotty knees with a skirt the size of a tent. He laced a bodice over his belt of strength and concealed his iron gloves beneath white mitts. Finally, Freya hung her necklace of starry jewels about his neck.

Yet Loki was not satisfied. "Whoever heard of a bride with red whiskers?" he asked, and persuaded Thor to shave off his beard.

Last of all, Thor took off his battle helmet and hid his fiery eyes beneath a bridal veil.

"Enchanting!" Loki giggled. "I'm speechless."

"You'd better be!" Thor growled. "If you say another word . . ."

"No bride growls so. Better take some honey to sweeten your voice. Or . . ." Loki did a handstand. "Better yet, take me along! I shall come as your handmaiden and speak for you."

So, with Thor dressed as the bride and Loki as the brides-maid, the two gods climbed into Thor's chariot and set off for Jotunheim. Although the goats, Gaptooth and Crack-tooth, galloped so fast that sparks flew like shooting stars from beneath their heels, the journey took eight days.

Thrym was waiting eagerly. As the chariot rolled to a stop, he lifted out his bride.

"Oof!" the giant wheezed. "How heavy you are for a maiden!"

Loki said quickly, "She's not too heavy for a big, strong giant like you."

Pleased, Thrym led them into his great hall. Mist clouded the ceiling, icicles dripped from the rafters, and torches held

in reindeer horns threw dancing shadows on the walls. Giants, wrapped in wolf skins, stood around tables heaped with food. Platters the size of sailing ships held roasted boars and oxen, and puddings as big as feather-beds overflowed their bowls.

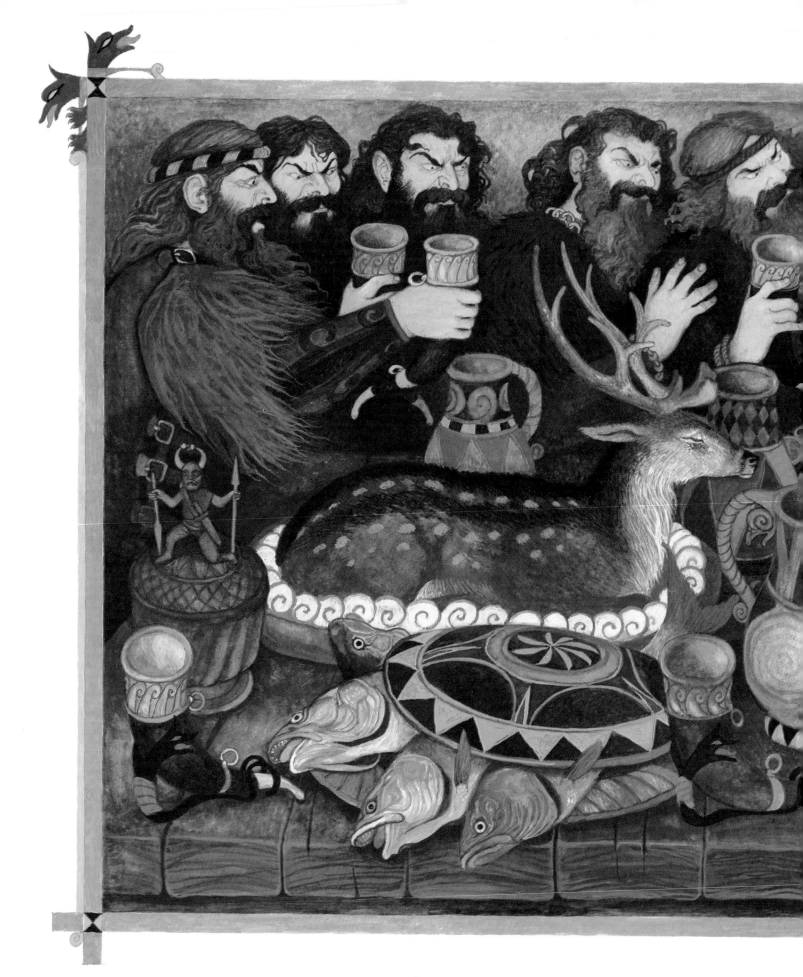

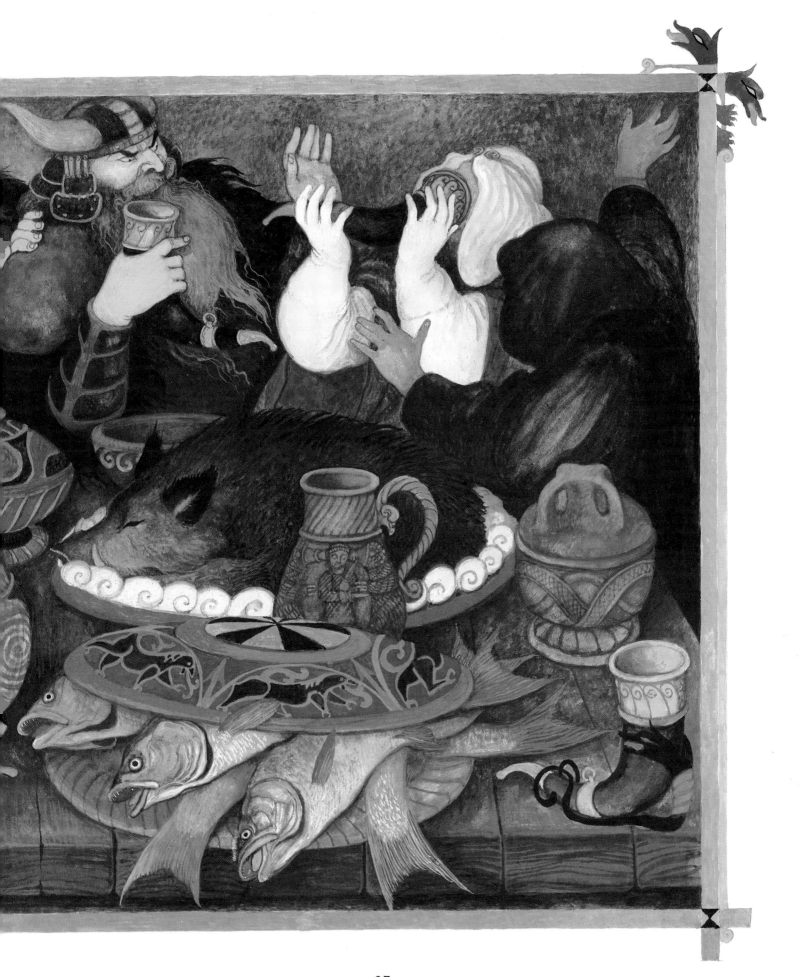

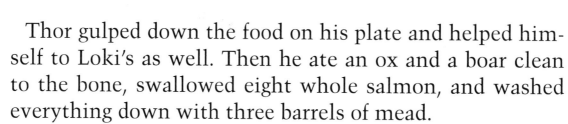

Thor gulped down the food on his plate and helped himself to Loki's as well. Then he ate an ox and a boar clean to the bone, swallowed eight whole salmon, and washed everything down with three barrels of mead.

"Are brides always so hungry?" wondered Thrym. "Never have I seen a maiden take bigger bites."

Thor hiccuped and loosened the laces of his bodice.

Loki was quick to answer. "Freya was so anxious to be your bride that she could neither eat nor drink for the eight days of our journey."

Pleased, Thrym said, "Now that she has dined, I must kiss my bride." He lifted Freya's veil and Thor glared at him with burning eyes. The giant jumped back. "Why are your eyes so red and angry, Freya?"

Loki answered, "Freya so longed to be here, she could not sleep for eight nights."

Pleased, Thrym clapped his hands and ordered, "Then on with the wedding!"

"First keep your bargain!" cried Loki, alarmed. "Trade Mjolnir for fair Freya."

The giant squinted down at Loki. His bride's talkative handmaiden seemed strangely familiar. But he shrugged and said, "Here is your wedding gift, my sweet." As he placed the hammer in Thor's lap, Thrym warned, "Watch out! Don't burn your pretty fingers!"

Thor seized Mjolnir. "Watch out yourself!" he roared, and hurled the hammer. Thunderbolts rocked the hall,

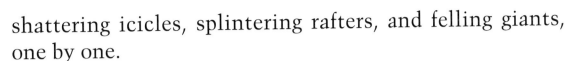

shattering icicles, splintering rafters, and felling giants, one by one.

Astonished, Thrym stood as if frozen.

Thor sprang to his feet, tore off the bridal veil, and shouted, "And here is Thor's gift to Thrym for stealing his hammer!" The last thunderbolt struck down the Frost King.

Then Thor strode over to Thrym's throne, placed a foot upon it, and declared,

> "I am the god Thor,
> I am the Thunderer.
> Here among icebergs
> Rule I the nations.
> This is my hammer,
> Mjolnir the mighty;
> Giants and sorcerers
> Cannot withstand it!
> Strength is triumphant,
> Over the whole earth
> Still is it Thor's-Day!"

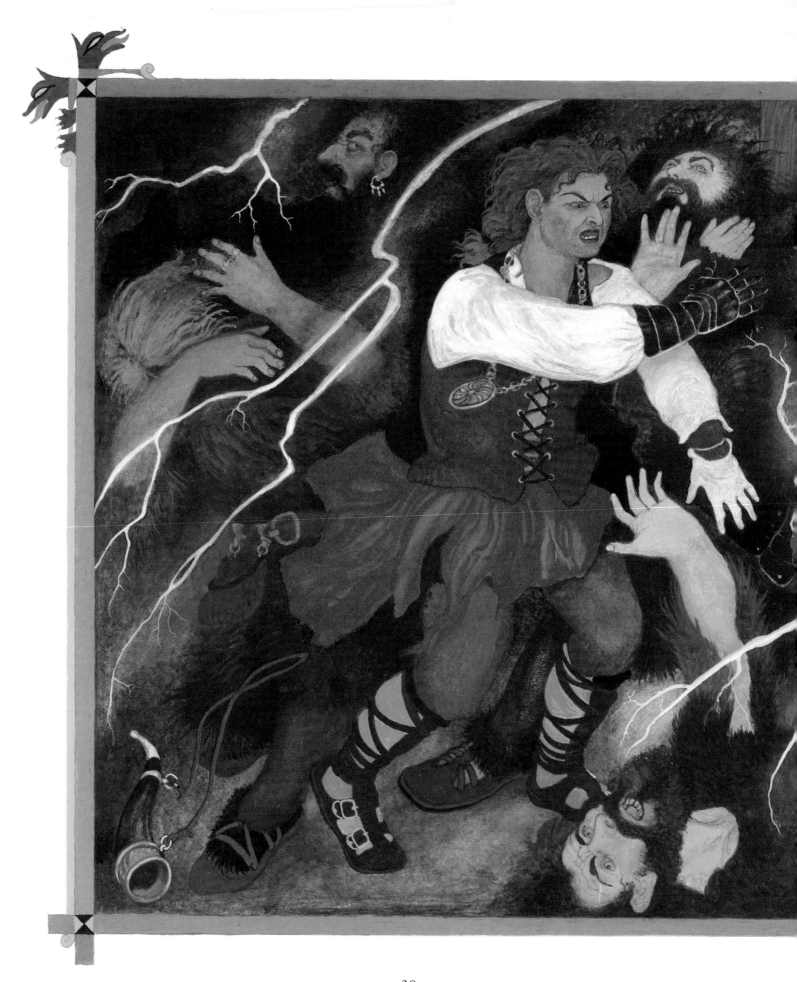

Thor and Loki harnessed the goats and trotted back to Asgard. When they reached the rainbow bridge, Thor climbed down from the chariot and threw his bridal dress high into the branches of the World Tree.

"Not a word about me or this foolish costume," Thor said sternly.

"Oh, never, Thor!" promised Loki. "I'll not tell anyone about Thor the beautiful bride."

Of course, Loki could not help dropping a hint here or whispering a word there, and soon everyone in Asgard knew what had happened. That's how, long ago, the Norse heard the story of Stolen Thunder. And that is why we can tell the tale today.